Cara
the Camp
Fairy

D1166799

Special thanks to Tracey West

If you purchased this book without a cover, you should be aware
that this book is stolen property. It was reported as
"unsold and destroyed" to the publisher, and neither the author
nor the publisher has received any payment for this "stripped book."

No part of this work may be reproduced, stored in a retrieval system,
or transmitted in any form or by any means, electronic, mechanical,
photocopying, recording, or otherwise, without written permission of the
publisher. For information regarding permission, write to
Rainbow Magic Limited, c/o HIT Entertainment,
830 South Greenville Avenue, Allen, TX 75002-3320.

ISBN 978-0-545-31656-9

Copyright © 2011 by Rainbow Magic Limited.

All rights reserved. Published by Scholastic Inc.,
557 Broadway, New York, NY 10012, by arrangement
with Rainbow Magic Limited.

SCHOLASTIC and associated logos are trademarks
and/or registered trademarks of Scholastic Inc. RAINBOW MAGIC is a
trademark of Rainbow Magic Limited. Reg. U.S. Patent & Trademark Office
and other countries. HIT and the HIT logo are trademarks of
HIT Entertainment Limited.

12 11 10 9 8 7 6 5 4 3 2 1   11 12 13 14 15/0

Printed in the U.S.A.   40
First printing, May 2011

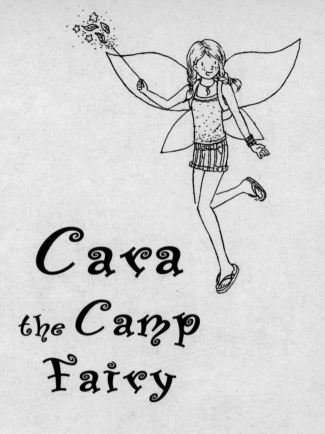

Cara the Camp Fairy

by Daisy Meadows

SCHOLASTIC INC.

New York Toronto London Auckland
Sydney Mexico City New Delhi Hong Kong

The Fairyland Palace

Craft Cabin

Mess Hall

Fire Pit

Sleeping Cabins

CAMP OAKWOOD

Camp Chaos!

Camp has things that goblins adore,
Bugs and games and sticky s'mores.
But I, Jack Frost, can't stand the sun.
I sit in the dark while campers have fun.

So I'll ruin camp and drain the lake.
I'll spoil the crafts kids love to make.
As long as I have the items three,
No one will have fun — except for me!

**Find the hidden letters in the leaves
throughout this book. Unscramble all 8 letters
to spell a special camp word!**

Contents

Goblin Tracks

"I can't believe we're actually at summer camp together!" Rachel Walker said happily.

"Me, neither," said her best friend, Kirsty Tate. "We get to do some of our favorite things all in one place. And we get to do them together!"

Rachel and Kirsty had met on

1

vacation on beautiful Rainspell Island.
Since they lived in different towns, they
didn't get to see each other every day.
So when the girls' parents had suggested
they go to Camp Oakwood, both
Rachel and Kirsty were excited.

Now, on their second day of camp,
the two girls sat at a table in the Craft
Cabin. They were making pictures
with yarn.

"First, sketch your picture on the
paper," explained Bollie, their
camp counselor. Bollie's
real name was Margaret
Bolleran, but everyone
called her Bollie.
Rachel sketched a fairy on her
paper. She looked over at Kirsty
and saw that she had sketched

a fairy, too. The girls smiled at each other.

"Now spread the glue over the places
you would normally color in," Bollie said.
"Then you can curl up pieces of yarn and
place them on the glue, like this."

She held up a picture of a tree with
green yarn for leaves and brown yarn
on the trunk . . . but then the yarn slid
off and plopped on one of Bollie's boots.

3

"That's weird," she said, feeling the paper. "This glue isn't sticky at all."

"My glue isn't sticking, either," complained a red-haired girl.

Bollie frowned. "Maybe it's too hot," she said, pushing her blonde bangs out of her eyes. "I know! Let's have some fun with the paint spinner, instead."

Bollie walked to a big machine on a table on the side of the room. Rachel,

Kirsty, and the other girls gathered
around to watch.

"It's easy," Bollie said, her green eyes
shining. "You put paper on the bottom.
Then you turn on the
spinner and
squeeze in
drops of
paint."
She held a
plastic bottle of
orange paint
over the spinner
and squeezed it.
With a *pop*, the
cover slipped off!
Instead of a few
drops, the whole bottle of paint gushed
into the spinner.

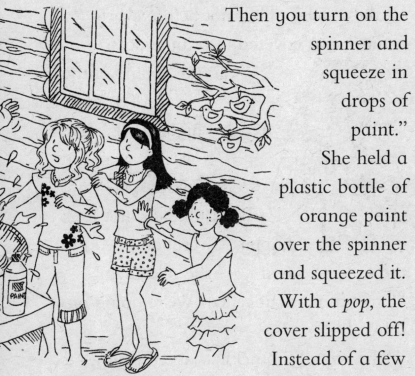

5

"Everybody duck!" Bollie yelled.

Rachel and Kirsty ducked down as quickly as they could. Orange paint splattered everywhere! Bollie turned off the machine, but not before every camper was covered in orange dots.

"Oh, no!" some of the girls wailed. Rachel giggled. "It's like we're covered in sprinkles," she said. But Bollie did not look happy. "Everybody head to the sinks to clean up!" she told them. "Craft time is cancelled. We're going on a hike!"

The campers quickly washed off the paint and changed into clean green-and-white Camp Oakwood tank tops.

They lined up at the edge of the woods.

"Follow me, and stick to the path,"
Bollie advised them.

Rachel and
Kirsty hung
back at the end
of the line.

"Rachel, why
do you think

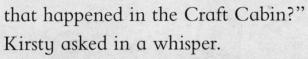

that happened in the Craft Cabin?"
Kirsty asked in a whisper.

Rachel gave her a meaningful look.
"It feels like Jack Frost to me."

Rachel and Kirsty were whispering
because they shared a big secret. They
were friends with the fairies! They
knew that wicked Jack Frost was always
playing tricks on fairies and humans
with the help of his goblins.

"But what would Jack Frost be doing at summer camp?" Kirsty wondered. "He likes to be in the cold, doesn't he?"

Just then, Bollie stopped suddenly on the path. "Look! Here are some tracks we can examine," she said.

The campers made a circle around Bollie as she bent down to give the tracks a closer look.

"That's strange," she said. "I thought maybe they'd be deer prints or raccoon tracks. But these look like big, bare feet. Who would walk around the woods in bare feet?"

Rachel and Kirsty knew exactly who would do that.

Goblins!

The Secret Switch

It was hard for Rachel and Kirsty to talk about the goblins, since they had to stay with Bollie and the other campers. They had to wait until dark, when everyone gathered around a fire for the nighttime story. They sat alone at a nearby picnic table.

"Did you see those tracks?" Kirsty

asked. "I'm sure that Jack Frost and his goblins are around here!"

"If they were causing trouble, wouldn't the fairies ask us to help?" Rachel wondered.

Kirsty nodded. "Maybe they don't know that Jack Frost is here."

Rachel frowned. "I wish we had some way to contact them."

"*Hmmm,*" Kirsty said. Then her eyes lit up. "We *do* have fairy dust!" The fairy dust was a present from King Oberon and Queen Titania, the fairy king and queen. Each girl carried some in a special locket. They could use the fairy dust to visit Fairyland.

"But we can't visit Fairyland now," Rachel pointed out. "It'll be time for bed soon. Bollie would be looking for us."

Kirsty was thoughtful. "Maybe we can sprinkle it on something," she suggested. "Like a mirror or a bubble. Something that would let us see into Fairyland."

Rachel pointed to a puddle at the foot of the rain barrel. "What about that?"

"Perfect!" Kirsty said.

The girls made sure no one was close by. Pale light from the moon shone on the puddle as Kirsty sprinkled some of her fairy dust.

A shimmery light beamed through the murky water, and then the faces of King Oberon and Queen Titania appeared.

"Hello, Rachel and Kirsty," said the queen. "What a pleasant surprise!"

"I'm afraid we have news that isn't so pleasant, Your Majesty," Kirsty said. "We think Jack

Frost and his goblins are here at Camp Oakwood."

The king and queen looked shocked. "We'll send Cara the Camp Fairy to help you right away," the king said. "Thank you so much," Rachel replied. Then the puddle went dark. A moment later, a small group of fireflies began to circle the girls. Their yellow lights blinked on and off. Then one of the lights got bigger and brighter.

The light exploded into a shimmer of
glittering sparks, like a mini-fireworks
display.

A fairy appeared in front of them! She
had freckled cheeks, two
sandy brown braids, a
colorful tank top, a cute
backpack, and shorts.
"Hey, campers!" she said
cheerfully. "I hear
you've had a goblin
sighting."

Kirsty waved hello to
Cara. "We saw goblin tracks!"

"And everything was messed up in the
Craft Cabin today," Rachel added.

Cara frowned. "That shouldn't have
happened. I have three magical objects
in here that help make camp extra-fun

for everybody." She slid her backpack off
and patted it.

"Ooh, can we see them?" Rachel
asked.

"Sure," said Cara. She flew to the
picnic table, opened up her backpack,
and dumped the contents onto the table.
Three big, gray rocks tumbled out.

"Oh, no!" Cara cried. "Jack Frost's

goblins must have stolen them!"

"Did you leave your backpack alone somewhere?" Kirsty wondered.

"No," Cara said, shaking her head. "But the other day I was in the woods near Jack Frost's palace when I saw some fairies camping out. They needed help, so I showed them how to build a fire. I put my backpack down for a few minutes."

"Those fairies must have been goblins in disguise," Kirsty guessed.

Cara nodded. "They must have secretly switched the magic items for rocks when I wasn't looking!"

"What do the magic items do?" Rachel asked.

"Each one helps give summer camp some extra sparkle," Cara explained. "My friendship bracelet helps make camp activities fun and exciting. My  water bottle helps keep campers cool in the heat. And my last item is a compass that keeps campers from getting lost."

"That must be why the paint splattered everywhere and the glue didn't stick," Kirsty realized.

"Right. Because the friendship bracelet is missing," Rachel said, finishing the thought.

Cara nervously flapped her wings. "We've got to find those goblins, fast!"

"Rachel! Kirsty!" a voice cried out just then.

Cara waved her wand. "Gotta go!"

The fairy disappeared as a little girl with short brown hair ran up. Kelly was a few years younger than Rachel and Kirsty, but she had latched onto them right away.

"It's time for lights-out!" Kelly told them. "But I'm not going to go to sleep

right away, are you? I'm going to read
my fairy book under the covers with my
flashlight."

"That sounds like fun," Rachel said.
"Kirsty and I like fairies, too."

Kelly beamed. "Aren't they the best? I
wish I could meet a real one."

Rachel and Kirsty smiled at each
other. They knew how lucky they were
to be friends with the fairies.

"I hope Cara comes back soon,"
Rachel whispered as they walked back
to their cabin.

"Me, too," Kirsty said. "If we don't get
those magic items back, summer camp
will be ruined!"

Camp Frost

The girls at Camp Oakwood slept in rustic wood cabins. Each one was filled with bunk beds. Rachel and Kirsty shared a cabin with five other girls their age. Their group was called the "Rowdy Raccoons."

The next day, after breakfast, the camp counselors gathered the Rowdy

Raccoons, the Cheerful Chipmunks, and the Silly Skunks by the sparkling lake. They were supposed to take a canoe trip. A row of canoes was tied to posts on the dock.

"*Hmm*. The lake looks a little low today," Bollie was saying to another counselor.

"It's deep enough for canoeing," said a different counselor, a woman with dark brown braids.

Bollie blew her whistle. "Okay, Rowdy Raccoons! We're taking these two canoes. Please put on your life jackets now."

"I've never been in a canoe before," said Kirsty, as she slipped on her orange vest.

"It's kind of like being in a sailboat, only we get to row," Rachel told her. "It's fun!"

Bollie and the other counselors stepped into their canoes first.

"Okay," Bollie said. "Please get into the canoe one at a time. No jumping, or you'll rock the boat!"

Rachel stepped in first. As she stepped

forward, her foot sloshed in a puddle of water.

"Bollie, is it supposed to be wet in here?" Rachel asked.

"Our canoe is leaking, too!" called another counselor.

"So is ours!"

Bollie shook her head. "It seems like nothing is going right today." She blew her whistle. "Okay, campers, you've got one hour of free time!" Rachel climbed out of the canoe. "My sneakers are squishy," she told Kirsty.

"It's because of the missing friendship bracelet," Kirsty said in a low voice. "Cara said its magic helps make camp activities fun and exciting. So far, almost every activity has been ruined!"

"Then I know how we should spend our free time," Rachel said. "We need to find Jack Frost."

Kirsty nodded. Then she noticed a bright glint at the edge of the woods. She nudged Rachel. "I think it's fairy magic. Look!" she said.

The girls ran toward the trees. As they got closer, they saw Cara sitting on an oak leaf, waving her wand.

"Thank goodness you

spotted me!" Cara said.

"We have an hour of free time," Kirsty told her. "We can help you look for Jack Frost."

"But I've already found him," Cara said, hopping off of the leaf. She grinned. "Jack Frost and his goblins are on the other side of the woods! He's set up his own summer camp."

"Why would he do that?" Rachel asked.

"Who knows?" said Kirsty. "But that's probably where he's keeping the magic objects!"

"Exactly," said Cara.

"We need to get there fast," Kirsty pointed out. "We don't have much time."

Cara waved her wand. "Then we'll fly!"

Shimmering clouds of fairy dust
sprinkled over the girls. They grew
smaller and smaller until they were
Cara's size. Wings sprouted from their
shoulders.

"Let's go!" Cara cried.

They flew quickly through the trees
until they came to the edge of the
woods. Then they stopped and hovered

with Cara behind a pine tree.

"See?" Cara said, pointing up ahead.

It looked like Jack Frost had taken over an abandoned camp. The big wooden sign used to say CAMP PINE TREE, but the words "Pine Tree" had been covered in green spray paint. Now the sign read CAMP FROST.

Goblins in Camp Frost T-shirts walked among the run-down cabins. Only one

of the cabins looked shiny and new,
glimmering with magic. Bright green
paint covered the walls, and a huge
air conditioner hummed in the front
window.

"That must be Jack Frost's cabin,"
Kirsty guessed. "He likes it best when it's
cold."

Then the girls heard a loud noise
coming from one of the other cabins.

It sounded like goblins yelling at each other.

"Follow me," Cara said.

The girls flew quickly through the camp. Then they stopped on the dusty windowsill of the noisy cabin and peered inside.

"It's the goblin's craft cabin," Rachel whispered.

Paint, glue, glitter, Popsicle sticks, pom-poms, and lots of other craft supplies were stored on shelves around the room. A group of green goblins with long noses sat at a table, painting pictures. As usual, the goblins were arguing.

"That's my paintbrush!"

"No, I had it first!"

At another round table, some goblins were making yarn pictures—or trying to. They were squirting glue on each other and wrapping each other in yarn!

"Hey, their glue and paint seem to be working just fine," Kirsty noticed.

"The friendship bracelet must be nearby," Cara said. She sounded excited.

She got closer to the window.

Rachel spotted something glimmering

on a shelf inside a plastic bin of friendship bracelets, colored string, and beads. She pointed it out to Cara. "That's it!" the little fairy cried.

"We have to fly past the goblins to get it," Kirsty said, sighing. "They'll see us."

Rachel thought hard. "I have another idea," she said. "The goblins are always putting on disguises to fool us. Maybe we can disguise ourselves to fool them."

"Disguise ourselves as what?" Kirsty asked.

Rachel grinned. "Goblins, of course!"

Cara's Crafty Magic

Cara clapped her hands together.
"That's perfect!"

"But where will we get goblin
costumes?" Kirsty wondered.

"Crafts are my specialty," Cara
explained. "And since we're close to the
special friendship bracelet, my crafty
magic should be working well."

Cara waved her
wand, and green
construction paper,
green yarn, and
tubes of green paint
appeared in front of her.
Then she waved her
wand again, and
gold stars and leaves
shot out as she sang a little song:

"Paper, yarn, and paint combine!
Make two costumes that are fine.
Rachel and Kirsty will be in disguise.
They'll look like goblins in everyone's eyes!"

The girls watched in amazement as
the different pieces came together to
make two goblin costumes: green shirts,

green pants, and long, green noses.
Cara waved her wand again, and the
costumes magically appeared on the
girls, who were back to their normal size
again!

Rachel and Kirsty stared at each other
for a moment.

"We look just like goblins!" Rachel
said with a giggle.

Cara smiled and crouched down on

the windowsill. "I'll keep watch. Good luck!"

Rachel and Kirsty were a little bit nervous. Fairies were nice—but goblins were another story.

The girls walked into the goblins' craft cabin. The goblins were still yelling and arguing as they tried to glue Popsicle sticks together.

"Jack Frost wants thirteen of these frames," barked one of the goblins. "So hurry up and make them!"

"But we don't know how," a goblin whined. "It's too hard."

Just then, the big goblin noticed Rachel and Kirsty. "Hey, you two!" he yelled.

The girls froze. Could he see through their disguises?

"What are you doing standing there? Make some picture frames!" he ordered.

"We'd better do what he wants," Rachel whispered.

The girls got to work, lining up the Popsicle sticks and gluing them together.

The goblin next to Rachel nudged her

with his bony elbow. "Hey, you know how to do it!"

"Sure," Rachel said, in a deep goblin voice. "It's easy. I'll show you."

The girls showed the goblins how to make the frames. Soon, they weren't arguing anymore. They were happily making crafts.

"This camping stuff isn't so bad," one of the goblins remarked.

"You're right," agreed his friend. "When Jack Frost set up this camp I thought he had a brain freeze. But he was right when he said that summer camp was fun."

"It's too bad he doesn't want to come

out in the sun with us," added another goblin.

The big goblin chuckled. "That's why we had to take Cara the Camp Fairy's magic items. If Jack Frost can't have fun in the sun, then nobody will!"

"So *that's* why he stole the magic items," Kirsty whispered to Rachel.

Rachel looked around. The goblins were still busy with their picture frames.

"Come on," she urged in a whisper. "Let's get that bracelet and get out of here."

The girls tiptoed to the shelf that held the friendship bracelets. Rachel saw the glowing bracelet, reached inside the bin, and slipped it into her pocket. It

shone with fairy magic.

The girls hurried toward the front door. But then one of the goblins took a step backward and bumped into Kirsty. Her fake nose slipped off!

The goblin gasped in surprise.

"Hey, these aren't goblins!" he yelled. "They're the girls who help the fairies!"

Rachel grabbed Kirsty by the arm. "Run!" she cried.

A Sticky Escape

"Don't let them escape!" the big goblin shouted.

The goblins raced to the door, blocking the way.

"Quick," Kirsty said, pointing to the back wall and shedding the rest of her goblin costume. "We can climb through that open window."

43

The girls darted for the window, and Rachel reached it first. She pulled herself up. But the goblins were right behind them. Would they make it?

"It's time to stop you goblins in your tracks!" a voice cried right then. It was Cara! She flew through the window and waved her wand. All of the glue bottles magically floated into the air. Then they turned upside down, dumping all of the sticky glue on the floor!

The goblins tried to lift their feet, but they were stuck in the goopy glue.

"We can't move!" the goblins yelled.

"Rachel, Kirsty, hurry!" Cara urged.

The girls quickly climbed out of the window and followed Cara to the woods.

Rachel looked behind her. Some goblins

from another
cabin were
chasing them
now!

Kirsty saw
them, too.
"Maybe we
can lose
them in
the woods!"

They soon
reached the
trees and
hurried down
the path.
They ran and
ran, with Cara
flying behind them.

"Camp Oakwood should be

just past those pine trees," Kirsty called out. But when they passed the pine trees, there were just more trees. Kirsty stopped to catch her breath. "That's weird," she said. "We should be at camp by now." "You're right," Cara agreed. "It feels like we're going around in circles." Kirsty slapped her forehead with her

hand. "That's it!" she cried. "Jack Frost still has the magic compass, which keeps campers from getting lost."

Cara started to fly up toward the trees. "I'll fly overhead and see where we are."

At that moment, a voice rang through the air. "Don't move!"

The girls froze. A dozen goblins emerged from the trees, surrounding them in a circle.

One of the goblins stepped forward. "Give us the magic friendship bracelet," he ordered.

"And what if we don't?" Cara asked.

"Why, we'll—*ow!*" the goblin yelled.

The rest of the goblins started crying out, too. *"Ow! Ow! Ow! Ow!"*

Cara started to laugh. "Look!"

A small army of chipmunks had

gathered around the goblins. They were
pelting the goblins with acorns!

"Run away! Run away!" one of the
goblins yelled.

The goblins scattered, and the
chipmunks scampered
over to Cara and the
girls.

"Thank you so much,

my friends," Cara said. "You know these woods very well. Can you help us get back to Camp Oakwood?"

The chipmunks made happy chirping sounds and ran ahead. The girls and Cara followed the cute little critters through the trees, to the edge of the woods by their camp.

"Thank you!" Rachel and Kirsty called as the chipmunks ran off.

Then Rachel reached into her pocket. "This belongs to you, Cara." She held out the magic friendship bracelet.

"Oh, thank you!" Cara cried happily. "All of the wonderful things I've heard about you girls are true."

She waved her wand over the friendship bracelet, and it shrunk down to fairy-size. Then Cara placed it in her backpack. "From now on, all the activities and games at camp will be fun," she promised.

"Rachel! Kirsty!"

The girls spun around. Kelly was running toward them.

Kirsty looked behind her. "Cara, you need to—"

But the little fairy was already gone.

Kelly's brown eyes were shining. "Did you see that thing with the glittery wings? I bet it was a fairy!"

"Are you sure it wasn't a butterfly?" Kirsty asked quickly. "There are a lot of pretty butterflies around here."

Kelly frowned.

"We can pretend it was a fairy, though," Rachel told the little girl. "Why don't we play a game? We'll go on a fairy search."

"I hope we find one for real!" Kelly said. She sighed. "I want fairies to be real so badly!" She ran ahead, toward camp.

"I wish we could tell her that fairies

are real," Rachel whispered.

"Jack Frost is real, too," Kirsty
whispered back. "We need to find the
last two magic items soon, so we can
start having fun at Camp Oakwood!"

Melting Magic

Contents

We're the Rowdy Racoons!

"Rise and shine, campers!"

The camp counselor's cheerful voice rang through the cabin. Rachel sat up slowly, rubbing her eyes. Kirsty put a pillow over her head.

"Is it morning already?" she asked.

"It's morning, and it looks like it's going to be a hot one," Bollie told them.

"But don't worry! We've got lots of fun things planned. Breakfast in fifteen minutes! I don't want my Rowdy Raccoons to be late."

Rachel hopped down from the top bunk. "Wow, Bollie's right," she remarked. "It feels very hot already."

"Well, it's summer. It's supposed to be hot," Kirsty said with a yawn.

The girls changed and headed to the mess hall with the rest of the girls from their cabin. Even though it was only the third day of camp, all of the Rowdy Raccoons had become friends. There was red-haired Brianna; Sophie with the freckles; Madison, who made everyone

laugh; and Alyssa and Abigail, the twins.

Inside the mess hall, the other campers were fanning themselves with their plates as they waited on line for breakfast.

"It's so stuffy in here," Rachel complained.

Kirsty pointed to the corner. "Look. I think the fans are broken."

Two of the camp counselors were

standing next to a big fan in the corner.
"It's plugged in, but it
won't turn on," one of
them was saying.
The girls looked
at each other.
"It's the missing water
bottle," Rachel
whispered. "Cara says
it helps keep campers cool in the heat."

"We're never going to cool off if we
don't get the water bottle back from Jack
Frost," Kirsty whispered back.

As the campers ate their eggs,
bacon, and cereal, Bollie made an
announcement.

"Attention, campers! The canoes have
been fixed. After breakfast, we're all
going to the lake so we can beat the

heat in the cool water!"

Everyone let out a cheer.

As soon as they finished eating, Kirsty, Rachel, and the other Rowdy Raccoons went back to the cabin to change into bathing suits and flip-flops. They came back outside carrying towels and bottles of sunscreen. Bollie was waiting for them.

"Excellent, Raccoons! You're the first ones changed. Line up and

follow me," she instructed.

Grinning, they all walked down the sunny path to the lake.

"I'm going to teach you your first camp cheer," Bollie called out. "After I sing a line, I want you to sing it back. Okay?"

"Okay!" the Rowdy Raccoons replied.

Bollie began the cheer, and the campers repeated after her.

"*Everywhere we go!*"
"*Everywhere we go!*"
"*People want to know!*"
"*People want to know!*"
"*Who we are!*"
"*Who we are!*"
"*So we tell them.*"
"*So we tell them.*"
"*We're the Rowdy Raccoons!*"
"*We're the Rowdy Raccoons!*"

"And if they cannot hear us!"
"And if they cannot hear us!"
"We sing a little louder!"
"We sing a little louder!"

The girls repeated the chant again and again, singing louder and louder each time. By the time they reached the lake, they were all giggling. They had almost forgotten how hot they were!

Suddenly, Bollie stopped marching.

"Hold on, everybody," she said, putting out an arm to stop the girls. "Something's not right."

She walked closer to the water and then turned back to the campers.

"The lake is even lower than it was yesterday," she said. "It's definitely too low to go canoeing, and it might not be

safe to swim."

Rachel, Kirsty, and the other Rowdy
Raccoons ran to the shore. Only a few
feet of water covered
the lake bed.

Rachel gasped.
"This is terrible!"

"And it's all Jack
Frost's fault!" Kirsty
whispered to her friend.

Can't Beat The Heat

By this time, the other campers had reached the lake, too. They all groaned when they saw how low the water was.

Bollie and the other counselors huddled together and talked in low voices for a minute. Then they clapped their hands and broke the huddle.

"Okay, campers!" Bollie announced.

"Looks like we won't be canoeing or swimming today. Please report to the camp courtyard for a water-balloon fight!"

All of the campers cheered.

"That sounds like fun!" Rachel said.

"And cool, too," agreed Kirsty. She lowered her voice. "I just wish we had a chance to go back to Jack Frost's camp."

"There's nothing we can do until free time," Rachel said. "But I bet Cara is trying to get the magic water bottle back right now."

"Rowdy Raccoons, line up!" Bollie called out. "Repeat after me: Everywhere we go . . ."

Rachel and Kirsty got in line as

the campers chanted and marched
away from the lake. Campers from
the other cabins joined in, too. The
chants got louder and louder as each
cabin competed to see who could be the
loudest of all.

The campers were hotter than ever
by the time they reached the courtyard
between the camp cabins. Bollie
marched them over to an outdoor faucet

on the back of the mess hall. One of the
other counselors came up and handed
her a bag of balloons.

"Let's do this in an assembly line,"
Bollie said. "Rachel and Kirsty, you fill
the balloons with water. Sophie, Alyssa,
and Abigail, you tie the knots. Madison
and Brianna, see if you can find a
bucket to hold the finished balloons."

Rachel turned on the faucet. She held
her hand under the water that trickled
out. It felt ice cold at first, and Rachel
splashed some on her face to cool off.
But when she put her hand underneath

again, the water was warm.
Rachel frowned. "I don't
think this water-balloon
fight is going to
cool us off."

The girls worked together to fill up all of the water balloons in the package. Soon they had a whole bucketful. Around the camp, girls from the other cabins were filling up their balloons, too.

"Okay, Raccoons, everybody grab as many balloons as you can," Bollie told them. "We're going to line up around the courtyard."

All of the campers formed a circle in the courtyard. Bollie blew her whistle.

"Let 'em fly!" she cried.

Rachel hurled a balloon across the courtyard. *Splat!* In landed in front of one of the Cheerful Chipmunk girls, splashing her with water. She laughed and tossed one back.

Splat! The balloon landed in front of Rachel and Kirsty, soaking them. But

instead of being cool and refreshing, the water was warm and uncomfortable. Yuck!

The excitement of the water-balloon fight quickly died down.

"Change of plans!" Bollie announced. "We're sending some of the counselors into town for some ice cream. You've got free time until they come back. I suggest you rest quietly in your cabins.

Play some checkers or read a book. It's too hot to do anything else!"

The soggy campers shuffled out of the courtyard. Rachel and Kirsty looked at each other and nodded. Instead of going to the cabins, they went right to the woods.

"I hope this is all right," Kirsty said worriedly. "Bollie said we should go to our cabins."

"She *suggested* it," Rachel pointed out. "That's different. Besides, we have to try to get that magic water bottle back. If we don't, we'll never cool off!"

"You're right," Kirsty said, nodding. "Let's go."

They easily found the path that led

through the forest. They followed it for
a while until the path forked in four
different directions.

Rachel frowned. "I don't remember
this."

"Me, neither," Kirsty said. "Let's pick a
path and see where it leads us."

The girls took the second fork on the
right and continued through the woods.

But they had to stop when the path forked again.

"I *definitely* don't remember this," Rachel said.

Kirsty's dark eyes got wide. "Oh, no! Remember what happened yesterday? Jack Frost has the magic compass that keeps campers from getting lost."

"And now we're lost again!" Rachel cried.

Cara to the Rescue!

Poof! Just then, Cara appeared in front of them. The air around her shimmered with fairy magic.

"Oh, girls, I'm so sorry!" she said. "I've spent all morning trying to get into Jack Frost's cabin. But now that he knows we're on to him, he has extra goblin security everywhere."

"Thanks for coming to our rescue,"
Kirsty said. "We were starting to think
we'd never find our way out of these
woods."

"I can fly above the trees and lead
the way," Cara told them. "But I don't
think there's any point in us going
to Camp Frost right now. We need a
different plan."

Kirsty looked thoughtful. "If we can't

get *into* Camp Frost, we have to get the goblins to come *out*."

"But how can we be sure they'll bring the water bottle with them?" Rachel asked.

Kirsty shrugged. "It's awfully hot out today. It seems like they'd carry water everywhere!"

"It won't be easy to get the goblins to leave camp, though," Rachel said.

Cara fluttered around the girls. "They're very anxious to get the friendship bracelet back again. We could use that to lure them out of their camp." She gave her backpack a worried pat. "But that could be dangerous. I'd hate to lose it again."

"There's lots of glittery thread in our Craft Cabin," Kirsty remembered. "We could make a fake friendship bracelet and fool them."

Rachel nodded. "Yes! We could bring a blanket to the edge of the woods and make friendship bracelets there. I'm sure the goblins will come sniffing around."

Cara looked excited. "And I can hide in the trees and surprise them! If one of

them has the magic water bottle, I can shrink it with my wand. Then I'll swoop down and grab it before they can stop me!"

"That's a great plan," Rachel agreed.

"But first we have to get back to camp, and we're lost," Kirsty reminded her.

"Not for long!" Cara sang out cheerfully. She flew up, up, up, above the trees. "Look in the sky and follow the fairy shimmer!"

The Trap is Set!

The girls looked up and saw what looked like a twinkling star shining over the trees. The star moved down the path, and the girls followed it. Within minutes they were back at camp, thanks to Cara!

"Wait here, Cara," Rachel told the fairy. "We'll get the stuff we need and hurry back."

As Rachel and Kirsty walked to the
Craft Cabin, they saw some of the camp
counselors pull into the
courtyard in a
minivan. One got
out of the passenger
side, opened the back,
and hauled out a big cooler.

"Ice cream! Get your ice cream!" she
called out.

Kirsty looked at Rachel. "Do you
think the ice cream is okay, or will the
missing magic water bottle ruin it?"

"There's only one way to find out,"
Rachel said, grinning.

They ran to the counselor and waited
in line to get their ice cream. The
counselor handed them each a wooden
spoon and a small cup with the words

CHOCOLATE ICE CREAM on the lid.

"Here goes," Kirsty said. She lifted off the lid.

"Uh-oh." Rachel looked into her cup and saw that the ice cream was bubbling!

"It's hot chocolate!" another one of the campers wailed.

"It's tasty, but it won't

cool us off," Kirsty said after taking a sip. She looked at Rachel. "We'd better hurry up with our plan."

They ran to the Craft Cabin and collected all the supplies they needed to make friendship bracelets: glittery thread, sparkly beads, scissors, two pieces of cardboard, and tape. Then they went to the Rowdy Raccoons' cabin and pulled a small picnic blanket from Kirsty's trunk.

Once they reached the edge of the woods again, Kirsty spread out the blanket. Both girls sat down and spread out the bracelet-making supplies.

Cara flew down from the trees, flapping her wings excitedly as she hovered between them.

"There are lots of goblins patrolling the woods, searching for the friendship bracelet," she said. "Maybe you could talk in loud voices about the bracelets. If they hear you, I bet they'll come running."

"Okay," Rachel said. She shivered a little, imagining the goblins running after them.

Cara saw her shiver. "Don't worry, Rachel. I'll be watching the whole time!"

"First, we need a bracelet that looks like the magic bracelet," Kirsty reminded her.

"Right!" Cara said. "Leave it to me." She waved her wand, and four pieces of glittery thread floated up above the blanket and began to twist around one another. Small, sparkly beads slid up the thread as the bracelet took shape.

Seconds later, the shimmering bracelet

floated back
down onto the
blanket.

"It's perfect!"
Rachel and Kirsty
cried at the same time.

"It's a good copy, but it doesn't have
any magic of its own," Cara said,
winking. "The goblins will be here soon.
I'd better hide!"

The fairy quickly flew up to her
hiding place in the trees.

Rachel chose one pink,
one blue, one yellow,
and one green thread.
She cut the threads so
they were as long as
the space from the tips of
her fingers to her elbow. Then

she tied the four threads together, at
the top. She taped the top to a piece of
cardboard to hold it in place and began
to weave the threads together, slipping
in glittery beads here and there.

"It's great that we can make crafts
again," Kirsty said in a loud voice.
"Thank goodness Cara gave us her
magic friendship bracelet!"

Kirsty expected the goblins to come
charging out at them, but things stayed
quiet and peaceful. It was a little bit
cooler under the trees, too.

"Boy, making friendship
bracelets is fun!" Kirsty
said, a little louder this time.
Then they heard something—
the sound of footsteps in the
woods, and the murmur of

goblin voices in the air.

"The sound came from over there!" one goblin said.

"Ugh, it's hot today," mumbled another.

A different goblin chimed in. "It's a good thing we've got the magic water bottle with us."

Kirsty glanced up at the trees. Did Cara hear that, too?

The goblins emerged from the path.

The girls could see a shiny water bottle that glittered with fairy magic hanging from a cord around a big goblin's neck.

"He brought it right to us," Kirsty whispered to Rachel.

Just then, the big goblin spotted the girls.

"Get the bracelet!" he ordered the others.

A Race through the Woods

As the goblins raced toward Rachel and Kirsty, Cara swooped down from the trees. She held her wand out in front of her, and it began to sparkle.

The big goblin was the first to spot her. "Grab her backpack! It's where she keeps the magic items!"

Kirsty picked up the fake friendship

bracelet. "No, we have the magic bracelet right here!" she cried.

But the goblins were determined to catch Cara. One of them jumped up and pulled the tiny backpack off her back.

"Woo-hoo! I got it!" he cheered, dangling the tiny backpack from his finger. Rachel knew she had to do something—and fast!

She charged at the goblin. He stumbled backward, and the backpack tumbled out of his grasp. Cara quickly grabbed it and flew out of reach as fast as she could.

"Cara, keep the backpack safe!" Kirsty called. "We'll get the water bottle."

The big goblin looked down at the
magic water bottle hanging around his
neck. "Oh, no you won't!" he promised.
Then he turned and ran, with the other
goblins right behind him.

"Come on!" Rachel called.
"We have to catch them
before they get back to
Camp Frost!"

The girls ran as fast as

they could, but the goblins were faster.
Leaves crunched under their feet as
they dodged around the
trees, trying to
catch up to the
goblin with the
magic water
bottle. Soon
the trees began
to thin out,
and the girls
realized they
could see the
cabins of Camp
Frost up ahead.

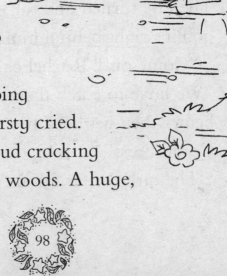

"We're not going
to make it!" Kirsty cried.

Just then, a loud cracking
sound filled the woods. A huge,

old tree branch crashed down across the path ahead! All of the goblins stumbled  over the fallen tree and piled up on top of each other. *"Ow! You're stebbing on by nose!"* one goblin complained in a muffled voice. "Get your elbow out of my ear!" yelled another. As the goblins struggled to get up, the magic water bottle slipped off of the big goblin's neck and rolled right toward the girls. Rachel quickly scooped it up.

"Rachel, look!" Kirsty said, pointing.

A furry brown beaver stood on her hind legs by the fallen tree branch. The beaver waved a friendly hello to the girls.

"She must be one of Cara's friends," Kirsty remarked.

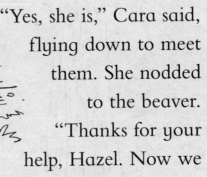

"Yes, she is," Cara said, flying down to meet them. She nodded to the beaver. "Thanks for your help, Hazel. Now we have to fly before those goblins untangle themselves!"

Cara waved her wand and turned the girls into fairies. Rachel held out the water bottle, and Cara put it in her backpack.

"After them!" the big goblin yelled, climbing to his feet.

Luckily, the girls could fly much faster than the goblins could run! They soared over the tops of the trees, leaving the angry goblins behind.

As they came to the edge of the woods, Kirsty spotted Kelly by their picnic blanket.

"Rachel! Kirsty!
Where are you?"
Kelly was calling.

"We'd better change
back," Rachel said,
fluttering her wings.

"Of course," Cara said. "And
thank you for helping me get the
magic water bottle. I think you'll find
that things at Camp Oakwood are
much cooler now."

The girls and Cara flew toward the
ground, making sure they were out
of Kelly's sight. Then Cara waved her
wand, and the girls changed back to
human-size.

"But we still have to find the missing
magic compass," Rachel reminded them.

Cara frowned. "I know. But I don't

think we should set another trap for the goblins. It's too dangerous."

"So what should we do?" Kirsty asked.

"I'm sure we'll think of something," Cara said brightly. "Campers are great problem solvers! In the meantime, go have some fun. Just be sure to stay out of the woods until we find the compass. I don't want you to get lost!"

Then Cara waved her wand and disappeared in a shower of sparkling fairy dust. Rachel and Kirsty emerged from the trees to find Kelly by the picnic blanket.

"There you are!" the little girl said. "Were you hunting for fairies? Because I saw some! I know I did!

And they weren't butterflies. I know because they were sparkly and shiny. They *had* to be fairies."

Had Kelly seen them flying with Cara?

Suddenly, they heard a loud cheer coming from the camp. The girls were happy for a distraction, since they couldn't tell Kelly their fairy secret! They rolled up the picnic blanket and ran toward the sound with Kelly alongside them.

All of the campers were racing down the path to the lake. When they reached the shore, Rachel and Kirsty saw what everyone was so happy about. The water level in the lake had risen! It looked nice and deep.

"Good news!" Bollie announced. "The water's back. Come get your feet wet!"

Kirsty and Rachel splashed into the lake. The water felt deliciously cool on their skin.

"Things are almost back to normal," Kirsty said.

Rachel nodded. "I can't wait until we get the magic compass back. We'll show Jack Frost that he can't ruin summer camp!"

Confused Campers!

Contents

Songs around the Campfire

"This ice pop is so cold, I'm getting a brain freeze!" Rachel cried, making a face.

Kirsty laughed. "This morning, I thought I would never feel cold again! So I don't mind a little brain freeze."

The girls were slurping on cherry ice pops in the mess hall. The other Rowdy

Raccoons were enjoying them, too. Madison was eating a grape one. She stuck out her tongue.

"Look! I'm turning purple!" she said, and everyone giggled.

"I'm glad it cooled off before the campfire tonight," said Sophie.

Brianna nodded. "We all would have melted!"

"I hope we get to sing some of the songs we sang last year," Sophie said.

"Kirsty and I don't know any campfire songs," Rachel told them. "It's our first time at camp."

"Oh, they're easy to learn!" Sophie said. Just then, Kelly ran up to the Rowdy Raccoons table. "Rachel!

Kirsty! Do you want to go look for
fairies now?" she asked.

"We'd love to play fairies with you,
but it's getting dark out," Kirsty told her.

Kelly looked sad.

"We can play tomorrow, okay?"
Rachel promised.

Kelly nodded. "Okay," she said softly,
walking back to the Sassy Squirrels'
table.

Kirsty leaned close to Rachel. "That reminds me," she whispered. "We should try to talk to Cara before the campfire starts."

The two girls got up. "See you later!" they called to the other Raccoons. Then they left the mess hall and walked to a quiet spot in a circle of pine trees. The setting sun cast shadows all around them.

"Cara, are you there?" Rachel asked.

Poof! The tiny fairy appeared in front of them, holding a stick with a marshmallow on top of it. "Hey!" she said with a smile. "I was just about to roast some marshmallows. Is everything all right?"

"We're fine," Kirsty replied.

"And nice and cool, too," Rachel added.

Cara smiled. "King Oberon and Queen Titania were so happy to hear that we got the magic water bottle back."

"But Jack Frost still has the compass," Kirsty reminded her.

"I know," Cara said with a nod. "But going after goblins in the dark is never a good idea. Tonight, you two should have some fun at camp."

"We're having a sing-along around the campfire," Rachel told her.

Cara's eyes lit up. "Oh, I love sing-alongs!" she said. "Do you think I can come?"

"You'd have to hide," Kirsty pointed out.

Cara looked thoughtful for a moment. Then she snapped her fingers. Her whole body began to glow. At the same time, she got smaller and smaller. Soon she was no bigger than a firefly!

She flew to Kirsty and landed right on the tip of her nose. "What do you think?"

"You look just like a firefly!" Rachel said.

"It's a great disguise, but you're making my nose tickle," Kirsty said, giggling. "I think I'm going to sneeze!"

"Sorry!" Cara said. She flew off of Kirsty's nose and zoomed between the girls, making swirls of light in the air.

The girls walked back to the center of camp, where the other campers were starting to gather around a bright, orange fire. The sky above was a deep blue, and the first stars were starting to twinkle. Rachel and Kirsty sat on a log next to each other. Kirsty felt Cara land on her shoulder.

"Okay, campers," Bollie announced. "It's time to sing!"

She started to sing in a loud voice,
and the other campers joined in:

"*The more we get
  together,
Together, together.
The more we get
  together,
The happier
  we'll be.*

*For your friends
  are my friends,
And my friends
  are your friends.
The more we
  get together,
The happier
  we'll be!*"

After a while, Rachel and Kirsty joined in, too.

"Sophie was right," Kirsty said. "It's easy!" They sang song after song. Kirsty could hear Cara's tiny voice singing along in her ear. By the time they sang the last song, the sky was black and a bright moon shone overhead. Bollie stood up. "It's time to hit the sack, campers!" she announced. "Cabins, please line up!"

Rachel and Kirsty got in line with the other Rowdy Raccoons. Bollie walked up and started to count them.

"Alyssa, check. Abigail, check. Brianna, check . . ."

Suddenly, one of the other counselors let out a yell.

"Oh, no! One of the Sassy Squirrels is missing!"

A murmur of alarm went through the campers. Bollie frowned and walked over to the counselor. "Who's missing?" she asked. "It's Kelly!" the counselor cried.

The Search for Kelly

Rachel and Kirsty gasped.

"She was at the campfire, I'm sure," the counselor said. "She must have wandered off."

One of the other little girls in the Sassy Squirrels cabin tugged on Bollie's shirt.

"I know where she went," the girl said. "She said she was going into the woods

to look for fairies."

"Oh, no!" Rachel turned to her friend. "Kirsty, if she's in the woods, she's going to get lost."

"Cara, what should we do?" Kirsty whispered.

But then she realized that she didn't feel Cara on her shoulder anymore. She looked around, but the fairy was gone.

"Maybe she's looking for Kelly," Rachel guessed.

"I hope so," Kirsty said. "We should look for her, too."

But Bollie blew her whistle. "I want all campers in their cabins right now! Counselors, when everyone is safely inside we're going to form a search party."

The girls had no choice. They marched
back to their cabin.

The other Rowdy Raccoons were
worried, too.

"I hope Kelly will be all right," said
Abigail.

"I'm sure the counselors will find her,"
Brianna chimed in.

Rachel and Kirsty looked at each
other.

"Jack Frost has the magic compass,"

Kirsty said in a low voice. "That means the counselors are going to get lost, too!"

"I know," Rachel said. "We have to help!"

Rachel and Kirsty didn't want to

disobey their camp counselor. But this
was an emergency! While the other
girls in the cabin talked and changed
into pajamas, they tiptoed out of
the cabin.

The girls hurried toward the woods.
They could see the yellow glow of
flashlights as Bollie and two other
counselors searched the trails.

"Kelly! Where are you?" the counselors called out.

A bright firefly flew toward Rachel and Kirsty in the dark, growing bigger and bigger as it got closer. But it wasn't a firefly at all—it was Cara!

"Sorry I left so quickly, but I was hoping to find Kelly before she got too far," Cara explained, looking serious. "I haven't found her yet, but I did find someone who can help."

As she spoke, a huge owl swooped down from the sky and landed on a nearby tree branch. The owl had golden feathers. His yellow eyes glowed brightly in his face.

"This is Midnight," Cara said. "He can see at night, so he'll help us find Kelly. But you two will need to fly."

She took some fairy dust from her
backpack and poured it into her palm.
Then she blew on it, sprinkling glittery
sparkles all over the girls. They quickly
turned into fairies!

The girls and Cara flew over to
Midnight and sat on his back. The bird's
feathers felt soft
but strong
under their
fingers. They
held on tightly as
the owl took off,
soaring high above the trees.

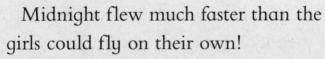

Midnight flew much faster than the
girls could fly on their own!

"This is a little scary!" Kirsty cried,
as the air pushed her braids straight out
behind her.

Rachel grinned and cheered. "I wish we could go this fast all the time!"

Just then, Midnight began to fly in a circle. He had spotted Kelly!

"There she is!" Cara cried, pointing down. The scared little girl was sitting at the base of a tree, crying. "Midnight, please let us down nearby. We can't let Kelly see us yet."

The owl slowly flew down to the forest floor. Rachel and Kirsty hopped off of his back.

"Thank you, Midnight," Kirsty said.

"I'll change you back," Cara told the girls, waving her wand. "Go get Kelly, and then look for Midnight in the trees. He'll lead you safely back to camp."

The girls nodded and ran off toward the sound of Kelly's sobbing. Her face

brightened when she saw them.

"Rachel! Kirsty! You found me!" she cried, jumping to her feet. She threw her arms around Rachel. "I was looking for fairies, but I didn't find any. Then I got lost!"

"You're not lost anymore," Rachel said. "Come on, let's get back to camp."

Kirsty heard a rustle and saw that Midnight had landed on a tree nearby.

"It's this way," Kirsty said.

The girls followed Midnight down the path. The owl flew quietly and slowly ahead of them, showing them the way.

After a few minutes, they heard voices up ahead and saw the glow of flashlights. Bollie and the other two counselors were arguing about which way to go. Then Bollie spotted the girls coming down the path. "Oh my gosh! Kelly!"

Kelly ran up to Bollie and hugged her.

"I'm so glad you're safe!" Bollie said. Then she nodded to Rachel and Kirsty. "What are you two doing out here?"

"We heard Kelly crying from our cabin," Kirsty said, thinking quickly.

"So we ran toward the sound," Rachel added.

Bollie frowned. "I know you were just trying to help. But you should never come into the woods at night. What if you had gotten lost, too?"

"Speaking of which," said one of the counselors, "how do we get back to camp?"

Kirsty spotted Midnight down the path

on the right. "I'm pretty sure it's this way. Follow me."

Thanks to Midnight, all of the girls got safely back to camp. Rachel and Kirsty went right to the Rowdy Raccoons cabin, but before they went inside, they looked up at the sky. Midnight was circling overhead, and a tiny bright light followed behind him.

"Thanks, Midnight," Rachel whispered.

"You, too, Cara," Kirsty added.

Get that Compass!

Rachel and Kirsty talked quietly together at breakfast the next morning.

"Kelly could have gotten hurt in the woods last night," Rachel said with concern.

Kirsty nodded. "Jack Frost has gone too far. It's one thing to spoil everyone's fun, but now he's putting

some campers in danger!"

After breakfast, Bollie made an announcement.

"In one hour we'll be starting our volleyball tournament," she said. "You have free time until then."

"Perfect!" Kirsty said to Rachel.

They put away their breakfast dishes and raced to the edge of the woods.

"Cara? Are you there?" Rachel called out.

They heard a noise from one of the trees and looked up to see Cara chatting with a robin on a branch. She flew down when she saw the girls.

"I had a feeling I'd see you two this morning," she said, smiling.

"We need to get back that magic compass, fast!" said Rachel.

"I know," Cara said. "But the goblins are guarding Jack Frost's camp. It won't be easy."

"Still, we have to try," Kirsty said.

"Now that's what I call camp spirit!" Cara cried. "Follow me, girls! Midnight helped me make a trail last night."

She pointed her magic wand at the path. Glittery craft beads lined the trail.

"See? We just follow the beads!" Cara said happily.

The path took them right to Camp Frost. But before they could hide, they heard a voice above them. "Those girls are back! Everyone to your positions!"

"Oh, no!" Cara cried. "Jack Frost has goblin guards in the trees!"

A small army of goblins ran out of the cabins. Each one held a slingshot, and they started shooting acorns at the girls!

"Run!" Rachel yelled.

The girls ran as fast as they could, with Cara flying right behind them. They didn't stop until they reached the edge of their own camp.

"That was close," Rachel said, catching her breath.

"You're telling me," Kirsty said. "We need a way to get past those goblin guards."

"But for now, you girls had better get back to camp," Cara told them. "I'll meet you back here when you have more free time."

Rachel and Kirsty nodded and waved as they ran off.

Back at camp, they found Bollie playing with Kelly and some of the young campers on the playground. Kelly was telling the others about her adventure the night before. "I didn't see any fairies, but I saw another camp on the other side of the woods," Kelly was saying.

"There were a bunch of boys wearing green uniforms."

Rachel nudged Kirsty. Kelly must have seen the goblins!

"That sounds like a Forest Scout camp," Bollie said. "There used to be a boys' camp on the other side of the woods, but it closed years ago. They must have reopened it." The camp

counselor smiled at Rachel and Kirsty. "I remember when I was your age. The girls raided the boys' camp with water balloons. That was a lot of fun."

"That does sound like fun," Rachel agreed, grinning.

Bollie snapped her fingers. "I've got it—we should raid the Forest Scouts today!"

"Oh, no," Kirsty said under her breath. She looked at Rachel with wide eyes.

If Bollie carried out her idea, she would be leading the campers right to Jack Frost and his goblins!

Girls vs. Goblins

"Are you sure that raiding the boys' camp is a good idea?" Kirsty asked nervously.

"Of course!" Bollie said. "It's a summer camp tradition!"

Rachel pulled Kirsty aside. "Maybe it's not so bad," she whispered. "There are lots of goblins, and only you, me, and

Cara to face them. If all of the girls here raid the camp, we might be able to get past the goblin guards. Then we could get to the magic compass."

"But then everyone will know that goblins are real," Kirsty reminded her. Rachel frowned. "I forgot about that." Kirsty was thoughtful. "You know, the goblins look a lot like regular boys when you first see them. Maybe we could do the raid when it's starting to get dark, so none of the girls can see them very well."

Rachel nodded. "Good idea!"

The girls walked back over to Bollie.

"A raid *would* be fun," Kirsty said. "What if we do it around sunset tonight?

That will give us time to plan."

"That sounds great," Bollie agreed. "We can figure out our strategy this afternoon."

"And we know how to get to the boys' camp," Rachel quickly added, thinking of the trail of beads. "We saw it last night when we found Kelly."

"Perfect!" Bollie said.

The next few hours went by like a regular camp day. They played volleyball, ate lunch, and started weaving potholders in the craft cabin. Then Bollie called all of the older campers together for a meeting in the mess hall.

"Here's the plan," she said. "The Forest Scouts have a camp on the other side of the woods. Right after dinner, we're

143

going to raid them. We'll run up to the
camp, pelt them with water balloons,
and then make a run for it." She held
up a brown grocery bag filled with
packages of balloons. "We've got a lot of
balloons to fill!"

The Rowdy Raccoons set up next
to an outdoor faucet and started an
assembly line, filling up balloon after
balloon. When they had no empty

balloons left, Rachel and Kirsty walked around the back of the mess hall.

Before they could call Cara's name, the fairy appeared in front of them. Her wings now looked like the wings of an orange-and-black butterfly!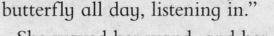

"I know about the plan," she said. "I've been disguised as a butterfly all day, listening in."

She waved her wand, and her wings turned back to their normal color.

"Bollie is a great counselor," Cara went on. "This plan is just what we needed! While the goblins are dodging water balloons, the three of us can go look for the magic compass."

The fairy winked and disappeared, and the girls headed into the mess hall for dinner. Everyone was so excited about the raid that they could barely eat their chicken and mashed potatoes!

When dinner was all cleaned up, Bollie blew her whistle. "Rowdy Raccoons, Silly Skunks, and Cheerful Chipmunks, please line up for the big raid!"

The older girls clapped and cheered.
Bollie motioned to Rachel and Kirsty.

"You two, front of the line," she said.
"We need you to lead the way."

The other campers grabbed buckets
of water balloons and lined up behind
Rachel and Kirsty. They walked to the
woods and then headed down the path
lined with glittering beads.

"Can we sing a camp song?" Madison asked.

"Not this time," Bollie told her. "We want this to be a surprise."

"It won't be much of a surprise if those goblin guards are still in the trees," Kirsty murmured to Rachel.

Soon they came to the trail near Camp Frost. Rachel and Kirsty looked up. There was no sign of the goblin guards yet.

"Luckily, goblins are lazy," Rachel told Kirsty in a low voice. "They must be taking a break."

Kirsty turned to Bollie. "We'll go up ahead and scout things out."

The two girls carefully made their way along the path. Through the trees, they could see goblins outside the cabins.

They were playing volleyball—or
trying to!

"*Ow!* You threw the ball at my nose!"
one goblin complained.

"It slipped out of my fingers!" another
goblin protested.

"They're arguing! Perfect," Kirsty said,
just as Cara appeared in a cloud of sparkles.

"Are we ready to go?" Cara asked.

The girls nodded.

"I'll go tell Bollie," Rachel said,
running back down the path.

A few seconds later, Bollie and the
other campers came jogging toward
Camp Frost.

"Camp Oakwood is the best! Better
than all the rest!" Bollie chanted. The
other girls joined in.

The goblins froze. They stopped

arguing and looked toward the forest.
Then . . .

SPLAT! The water balloons started
flying!

"Oh, no! It's *clean* water!" a goblin
yelled. "Yuck!"

"Run for cover!" the other goblins
cried. They started dashing around the
camp, bumping into one another.

Rachel and Kirsty knew they had

to act fast, while the goblins were distracted. They ran toward the cabins.

"I'm sure Jack Frost has the magic compass in his cabin," Cara said, appearing in the air next to them.

As they reached the main cabin, Rachel threw open the door. A blast of freezing cold air rushed out.

Just inside the door, a tall man with spiky white hair and a long, pointy nose faced them.

"Jack Frost!" Kirsty cried.

The wicked fairy held up his hand and opened his palm. The magic compass glittered against his pale skin.

"Are you looking for this?" he asked with a grin.

A Tricky Trade

Cara bravely flew right up to Jack Frost.

"Give that back!" she said firmly. "The magic compass doesn't belong to you."

Jack Frost just laughed. "It's mine now, little fairy!"

"But that compass keeps campers from getting lost," Rachel told him. "And last

night, Kelly got lost in the woods."

"She could have gotten hurt," Kirsty added. "That's just plain mean, Jack Frost!"

"Hmph!" Jack Frost scowled. "I just wanted to have fun camping, like everybody else!"

"Why can't you have fun camping?" Kirsty asked.

"Oh, I can make crafts and swim in a lake if I want to," Jack Frost replied, rolling his eyes. "But at night, campers sit around a campfire and roast marshmallows and sing songs. I can't do that, because the fire is too hot!"

"So you wanted to ruin everyone else's time at camp, just because you can't sit around a campfire?" Rachel asked.

Jack Frost nodded. Suddenly, he

reached out and grabbed Cara from
the air. "And now, I'll take back that
friendship bracelet and water bottle!"

Cara struggled to get free from Jack
Frost's grip. He reached for her backpack
with a long, pointy, finger.

"Wait!" Kirsty cried. "How about a
trade?"

Jack Frost stopped.
"What kind of trade?"

Kirsty raised an
eyebrow. "I bet Cara
could make you a
magic fire that feels
cold, not hot. Couldn't
you, Cara?"

The little fairy nodded. "Of course!
Campfire magic is one of my favorites!"

"With a magic fire, you and your

goblins could roast marshmallows and
sing campfire songs all night long,"
Kirsty told Jack Frost.

His pale eyes gleamed with
excitement. "That would be wonderful!"

"I'll only do it if you give me the
magic compass," Cara said. "Do we
have a deal?"

Jack Frost was silent for a moment.
Then he opened his palm and freed
Cara. "Deal!" he said.

Cara flew up into the air and waved
her magic wand. Glittery blue sparks
whirled around her as she began her
fairy spell.

"Fire, fire, burn so nice.
Burn with flames as cold as ice!"

Poof! A roaring campfire appeared
outside the door of Jack Frost's cabin.
He slowly walked up to it and passed his
hand over the flames.

"They're positively freezing!" he cried.
"How marvelous!"

"Now it's time to fill your end of the
bargain," Rachel reminded him.

Jack Frost held out the magic compass.

Cara waved her wand over it, shrank it down to fairy-size, and slipped it in her backpack.

"Come on," Kirsty said. "Let's go before he changes his mind." The girls ran outside to see the goblins still fleeing from the water balloons. They were all bumping into one another!

Then Bollie blew her whistle. "We're out of balloons, girls! Let's retreat!"

The girls turned and raced back down the forest path, hollering and squealing with excitement.

"I'll catch up with you later," Cara told Rachel and Kirsty, grinning from

ear to ear. "I'm going to tell the king and queen that we found the magic compass!"

The fairy vanished in a whirl of sparkles, and the girls chased after the other campers.

By the time they got back to camp, it was dark. Some of the other counselors had started a campfire.

"Great raid, girls!" Bollie said, catching her breath. "Let's celebrate with some s'mores!"

The campers gathered around the fire to make the tasty treats with toasted marshmallows, chocolate, and graham crackers.

"This is delicious!" Kirsty said after her first bite.

"I wonder if Jack Frost knows how to make s'mores?" Rachel asked with a smile.

The happy chatter of the campers filled the camp. Then, in the distance, the girls heard a strange howling.

"What's that?" Bollie wondered.

The girls got quiet as they listened. It sounded like boys singing in horrible, off-key voices.

"The more we get together,
Together, together.
The more we get together,
The nastier we'll be!"

Bollie shook her head. "Sounds like those Forest Scouts to me." Rachel and Kirsty looked at each other and grinned. They knew the truth. Those terrible singers were goblins!

The next morning, the girls woke to bright sunshine streaming through their

cabin windows. The other Rowdy

Raccoons were still asleep. Suddenly, a robin appeared at the window. She gently tapped her beak against the glass.

"That looks like Cara's friend," Kirsty said.

The two girls quietly went outside and sat on the cabin steps. Cara flew up to them.

"Rise and shine, campers!" she said cheerfully. "I have something for you."

Cara opened her backpack and took out three glittery friendship bracelets.

"Ooh, they look just like the magic bracelet!" Kirsty cried happily.

"There's one for each of you, and one

for Kelly," Cara said. "King Oberon
and Queen Titania felt just terrible when
they heard how she got lost."

"Thank you so much, Cara!" Rachel
said.

Cara gave each girl a kiss on the
cheek. "Thanks to you, campers
everywhere will have a great time this
summer!"

"Will we see you again?" Kirsty asked.

Cara nodded. "If you need me, just call my name. But right now, I've got to go referee a game of volleyball."

The fairy flew up toward the trees. The robin joined her, and the two of  them swooped and swirled in the sky. "See you soon, Cara!" Rachel and Kirsty called, waving. The girls spotted Kelly a little while later at breakfast. Rachel winked at Kirsty, then handed Kelly one of the special friendship bracelets.

"This is for you," she said. "It's just like ours, see?"

Kelly's eyes got wide. "It's so pretty! It

looks just like a magic fairy bracelet."
She stopped. "Do you think fairies are
real?"

Rachel and Kirsty smiled at each
other. They could never tell Kelly their
secret—but they didn't need to.

"They're real if you believe in them,"
Rachel said.

Kirsty nodded. "Rachel's right. If you
believe in fairies, they'll always be with
you."

Kelly smiled. "I knew it!"

RAINBOW magic™

There's Magic in Every Series!

The Rainbow Fairies

The Weather Fairies

The Jewel Fairies

The Pet Fairies

The Fun Day Fairies

The Petal Fairies

The Dance Fairies

The Music Fairies

The Sports Fairies

The Party Fairies

The Ocean Fairies

Read them all!

SCHOLASTIC and associated
logos are trademarks and/or
registered trademarks of Scholastic Inc.
©2011 Rainbow Magic Limited.
HiT and the HiT Entertainment logo are
trademarks of HiT Entertainment Limited.

www.scholastic.com

www.rainbowmagiconline.com

RMFAIRY3